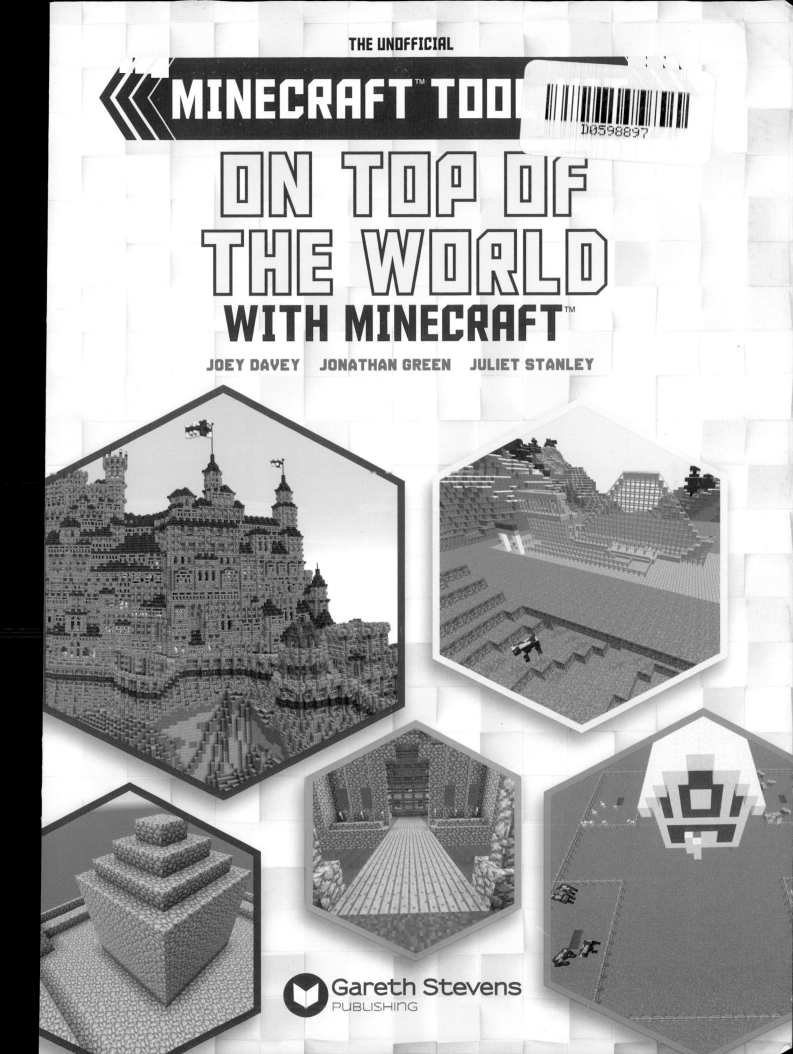

THE UNOFFICIAL

MINECRAFT™ TOOL

ON TOP OF THE WORLD
WITH MINECRAFT™

JOEY DAVEY **JONATHAN GREEN** **JULIET STANLEY**

Gareth Stevens
PUBLISHING

Please visit our website, **www.garethstevens.com**.
For a free color catalog of all our high-quality books,
call toll free 1-800-542-2595 or fax 1-877-542-2596.

Cataloging-in-Publication Data
Names: Davey, Joey. | Green, Jonathan. | Stanley, Juliet.
Title: On top of the world with Minecraft™ /
Joey Davey, Jonathan Green, and Juliet Stanley.
Description: New York : Gareth Stevens Publishing, 2018. |
Series: The unofficial Minecraft™ tool kit | Includes glossary.
Identifiers: LCCN ISBN 9781538217139 (pbk.) | ISBN 9781538217085 (library bound) |
ISBN 9781538217030 (6 pack)
Subjects: LCSH: Minecraft (Game)--Juvenile literature. | Minecraft (Video game)--
Handbooks, manuals, etc.--Juvenile literature. | Building--Juvenile literature.
Classification: LCC GV1469.M55 D38 2018 | DDC 794.8--dc23

Published in 2018 by
Gareth Stevens Publishing
111 East 14th Street, Suite 349
New York, NY 10003

Designed and packaged by: Dynamo Limited
Built and written by: Joey Davey, Jonathan Green, and Juliet Stanley

Printed in the United States of America
CPSIA compliance information: Batch CW18GS: For further information contact
Gareth Stevens, New York, New York at 1-800-542-2595.

CONTENTS

WELCOME
TO THE WONDERFUL WORLD OF
MINECRAFT!

If you're reading this then you're probably already familiar with the fantastic game of building blocks and going on adventures. If you're not, go download Minecraft now and try it out!

READY?

OKAY, LET'S GET STARTED!

Courtesy of IAmNewAsWell

《 THE AIM OF THE GAME 》

One of the greatest things about Minecraft – apart from being able to explore randomly generated worlds – is that you can build amazing things, from the simplest home to the grandest castle. This book will help you become a master builder, capable of building your own epic Minecraft masterpieces.

This book has projects of three different difficulty ratings, which will help you hone your building skills. Each project has clear step-by-step instructions. You'll also find expert tips, like this one . . .

Courtesy of crpeh

EXPERT TIP!

CREATIVE MODE vs SURVIVAL MODE

If you build in Creative mode, you'll have all the blocks you need to complete your build, no matter how outlandish. However, if you like more of a challenge, why not build in Survival mode? Just remember – you'll have to mine all your resources first, and you will also be kept busy crafting weapons and armor to fend off dangerous mobs of zombies and creepers!

FAIL TO PREPARE AND PREPARE TO FAIL

If you're building in Survival mode, before you get going, you'll need to set up your hotbar so that items such as torches, tools, and weapons are all within easy reach. You'll also want to make sure that you're building on a flat surface.

For the best results, use Minecraft PC to complete all of the step-by-step builds in this book.

Before you start, you'll need to mine all your resources, and before you can do that, you'll need to sort out your Tool Kit . . . turn the page for further help.

Courtesy of swifsampson

EXPERT TIP!

ALL THAT GLITTERS

If you're planning on creating a Minecraft masterpiece, you'll want some super-special materials. To find rare ores, like diamonds, mine a staircase to Level 14 and then strip-mine the area. But remember – you'll need an iron or diamond pickaxe to mine most ores. If you use any other type of tool, you'll destroy the block without getting anything from it.

Courtesy of Cornbass

STAYING SAFE ONLINE

Minecraft is one of the most popular games in the world, and you should have fun while you're playing it. However, it is just as important to stay safe when you're online.

Top tips for staying safe are:
» turn off chat
» find a kid-friendly server
» watch out for viruses and malware
» set a game-play time limit
» tell a trusted adult what you're doing

TOOLED UP!

Before you get cracking – or should that be crafting? – you're going to need to make sure that you're set with all the tools you'll need.

⟪ CUSTOMIZE YOUR HOTBAR ⟫

Your inventory is the place where everything you mine and collect is stored. You can access it at any time during the game.

When you exit your inventory, a hotbar will appear at the bottom of the screen, made up of a line of nine hotkey slots. Think of this as your mini-inventory where you can keep the things you use most frequently.

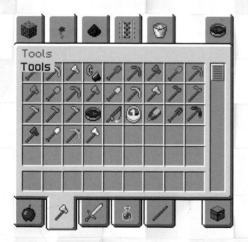

It's vitally important to take time to organize your hotbar carefully – in a game of Survival, it might just save your life!

Move an item from your inventory into one of the hotkey slots to assign it. Then, when you select a slot, the item you have placed in there will automatically appear in your hand, ready for you to use.

⟪ HOT OR NOT ⟫

Always keep at least one weapon and one food source in your hotbar. Also make sure you've got some tools in there. It's always handy to have a pickaxe or two, or perhaps a shovel, depending on what you're planning on mining. A torch will also be handy. Last of all, you want to make sure that you have some basic building materials ready.

EXPERT TIP!

GO FISH!

Fishing rods are surprisingly useful. You can use them to catch fish, and you can also cast them to set off pressure plates while you stay out of harm's way.

BUILDING BLOCKS

WOOD

Always useful, as you need it to craft many everyday items. In Survival mode, always carry some logs with you – especially if you're going caving, as wood is hard to find underground.

EXPERT TIP!

REDSTONE RAMPAGE

If you want your Minecraft masterpiece to have moving mechanisms, like a roller coaster, you're going to need some redstone. This block allows you to create moving parts, and even circuits.

STONE

The most common block in the game, it is good at keeping creepers at bay. If you're planning on building a castle, stone is what you're going to need – and lots of it!

BRICK

Harder than stone and can be crafted out of clay, although it does take a long time to craft and will drain your fuel supply.

OBSIDIAN

Other than bedrock, this is the hardest material – and it's completely creeper-proof! You'll need an entire lava source block and 15 seconds with a diamond pick to mine it in Survival mode, though.

MIND-BOGGLING BIOMES

The different types of terrain you encounter in Minecraft are called biomes. They range from ice plains and swamps, to deserts and jungles, to oceans and fantasy islands.

Courtesy of Epic Minecraft Seeds

Courtesy of MADbakamono

These biomes will take you to the sky and back, quite literally!

UN-BOX YOUR BUILD

The amazing world of Minecraft is made from lots and lots of . . . blocks! But these simple, straight-edged blocks certainly don't stop its biggest fans from building masterpieces that curve, spiral, and defy the cuboid. With a little help and a lot of imagination, you can make even your wildest dream builds come true. Let's take a look at some of the creative possibilities Minecraft has to offer.

❰❰ ECCENTRIC ENTRANCES ❱❱

Make your entrances unforgettable with lots of different materials, shapes, and a few surprises! The first door is the perfect entrance for a treetop lodge. From a distance it looks like it has been carved out of a tree trunk by woodland creatures. There's a hidden entrance in the second doorway, and the colors created by wool and emerald blocks are totally wild!

❰❰ WOW FACTOR WINDOWS ❱❱

Why not try your hand at making these stunning windows? Short rows, L-shapes, and single blocks create a circular web within the frame of the first window. Diagonally placed blocks in the second window create curved lines that look like a propeller. But you don't have to stick to square windows – anything is possible in Minecraft!

EXPERT TIP!

SKETCH IT

Being prepared will make building in Minecraft easier and much more fun. You'll have a good idea of what you want your final build to look like, and you'll have given yourself time to think about how to do it. Forget math for a second – grid paper is perfect for planning what to do with all of these blocks!

The dark blue flooring and back wall cleverly disguise this open entrance.

REMARKABLE ROOFS

Here are three in-spire-ational roofs for you to try! For a look inspired by ancient Chinese architecture, add blocks in the corners of simple roof structures. Or go for a space age design with lava, emerald, diamond, and beacon blocks! Staying hidden is always a good strategy in Survival mode – this last grass roof is the perfect way to disguise your builds.

SENSATIONAL STRUCTURES

Yes, it's a woolly hat house made from wool blocks! Try recreating this circular structure with lots of different-sized rows. The only rule is: stay symmetrical. This arched bridge is a super-simple structure, and it can be used to add interest to the front of a building, or to un-box square windows. The last building uses columns to support a balcony and to add texture to its surface. This would be a great look for a castle.

EXPERT TIP!

BE INSPIRED

Search online or flick through books to find inspiration for your creations! As well as a myriad of Minecraft buildings, you'll find plenty of weird and wonderful real-life buildings that you can use to help you come up with your very own masterpiece. Happy building, Minecrafters!

MOUNTAIN MUST-HAVES

What could look more impressive than a mountaintop fortress rising majestically out of snow-topped crags?

If you're planning on building your own mountain hideaway, don't peak too soon! Prepare yourself with these solid tips on how to succeed.

HOLDING A TORCH

EXPERT TIP!

Did you know that monsters can spawn just seven blocks away from a single torch, including inside your build? To keep hostile mobs out and stop your dream home from becoming a living nightmare, place torches no more than seven blocks apart in any direction. Surround the outside of your build with well-spaced torches, too, to keep horrors from spawning on your doorstep!

≪ BASE CAMP BUILDING ≫

When building in the mountains, there are a few DOs and DON'Ts to bear in mind:

» DO build your base with resistant materials.

» DON'T forget to dig yourself an escape tunnel – just in case!

» DO build several layers of defenses – everything from drawbridges to redstone-powered portcullis traps!

» DON'T forget to clear any surrounding forest to stop hostile mobs from creeping up on you.

» DO craft an iron door to keep zombies out, just in case . . .

≪ SUMMIT SPECIAL ≫

Mountains are really just hills with extreme slopes and cliffs. Dramatic overhangs can form and mountains sometimes have caves running through them. Take time to find the perfect place, and incorporate the landscape into your build, using ledges as part of your roof and turning holes in the hills into stunning rooms.

Courtesy of Planet Minecraft

EXPERT TIP!

PICK YOUR AXE

If you're going to be doing a lot of crafting using stone, and other similar materials, then you will need a super-strong pickaxe. Diamond is best! But did you know you can increase the toughness of your tool by combining two damaged ones to make a new one?

EXPERT TIP!

COBBLESTONE

Cobblestone is an excellent base material, even though it won't win any beauty awards. It will not catch fire when lightning strikes, and creepers will have a hard time trying to blast it away. So double the walls up for extra blast protection!

BACK TO BEDROCK

When you're building in the mountains, if you start digging down, sooner or later you're going to come up against a layer of bedrock. In Survival mode, bedrock cannot be broken using any tools at all. It cannot be moved by pistons, and it cannot even be destroyed by explosions.

FARM

DIFFICULTY
EASY

BUILD TIME
1 HOUR

Farming leads to Survival mode success because it gives you a constant energy source. Hostile mobs don't attack passive mobs, like farm animals, so you can farm safe in the knowledge you only have to look out for yourself. This is an animal farm, but there's nothing to stop you from growing fruit and vegetable crops in yours – and because it's Minecraft, you only grow the ones you like.

STEP 1

First fence off a large area of land – at least 35x35. Then build barn walls from red hardened clay, 13 blocks long, ten wide, and seven high. This barn is placed towards the back of the enclosure, but you can put yours wherever you like!

MATERIALS

STEP 2

Build up the front and back walls of your barn in a stepped manner in preparation for adding the roof. Remove 3x4 blocks to make a start on your entrance.

STEP 3

Five blocks up, replace the clay to make a quartz stripe around your barn. Build the roof from 15-block-long rows of quartz. You'll need six single-block rows and three two-block-wide rows. Position these so there's a one-block overhang at each end of the barn.

STEP 4

Decorate the front of your barn by replacing the red-hardened-clay blocks with quartz blocks, as shown. Use quartz blocks to create barn doors, too. Now you have a barn to build the rest of your farm around!

STEP 5

Inside your barn, build an oak-wood-plank platform five blocks up. This one is eight blocks long. Add torches, beds, hay bales, and anything else you think would make you feel more comfortable!

STEP 6

Build a column from oak wood plank and a ladder for easy access to your sleeping area. Then down below, add some more hay bales, torches, and some tamable mobs.

EXPERT TIP!

HAY!

Hay bales are a great way to break your fall – so how about customizing this build with a hay bale staircase? Hay bales can also be used to breed llamas, heal horses, and help foals grow, so it might be something you'd like to farm. Nine sheaves of wheat will craft one hay bale in Survival mode.

STEP 7

Back outside, build four corner paddocks from fence. Include some fence gate for easy access to your animals and provide water in each paddock. Then select the animals you would like to farm. Here are pigs, cows, sheep, and chickens.

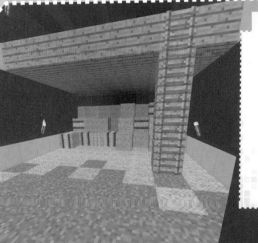

ON TOP OF THE WORLD

ROLLER COASTER

DIFFICULTY
INTERMEDIATE

BUILD TIME
2 HOURS

Time to go up in the world!
A roller coaster is the perfect way to enjoy some Survival time with your friends. This one even has space for hordes of waiting Minecrafters. If you're feeling ambitious, you can build your roller coaster in the mountains so that the drops and rises appear even more breathtaking. But before we get too carried away, let's start with some basic engineering . . .

MATERIALS

STEP 1

First build a base using 3x21 planks. Add a row of ten stairs on one side with a plank at each end. Construct a fence around your base, leaving gaps for the steps at one end.

STEP 2

Add one plank at the open end of your base and lay one rail and 20 powered rails. Build three extensions to your base for redstone torches. These power your ride, and when they go dark red you'll need to add more.

STEP 3

Up we go! Add two planks to the end of your base with five blocks stepping up from it. Connect this to a three-plank row, and you have created the first rise in your ride!

STEP 4

Add four planks to the right, turn right and add ten planks, then turn right again and add four planks. Build a four-plank diagonal rise up from this and connect it to a five-plank row, a four-plank row, and a ten-plank row so you have a shape like a spiral staircase.

STEP 5

Now you need to build a diagonal drop next to your ten-plank row. It should fit neatly between the rows and diagonal rises you have just created. Use eight two-plank steps to create this death-defying drop.

EXPERT TIP!

OPTICAL ILLUSION

Surprise your riders with a steep vertical drop followed by a gap and a false track that looks like it's the next part of your roller coaster but isn't. Your riders will be left wondering what is going to happen to them before they plunge down the vertical drop and the real ride continues!

STEP 6

Lay powered rails (standard rail corners for the turns) from the base of the roller coaster to the end of the second level. Then add planks with torches on top to the outside edges of the roller coaster to power it.

STEP 7

Build a four-plank square at the bottom of the drop and a seven-plank row leading back to your base. Add a one-plank step up, another four-plank row, a two-plank row, and a massive 11-plank diagonal rise, as shown.

STEP 8

Attach a seven-plank row to your diagonal. Build a ten-plank diagonal drop followed by a six-plank C-shape. Add a diagonal drop made from three sets of two-plank rows. Link this to your base with four planks.

STEP 9

Lay powered rail to the fourth plank on the last diagonal rise, then standard rail to the top and all the way back down to your base. Now strengthen your roller coaster by adding fence to the underside of each diagonal.

STEP 10

Keep adding fence to the space between the top level of your roller coaster and the base until it is completely filled. Build fence from the ground at each end of the base up to the top level on all sides.

STEP 11

Now lay paving using stone brick and erect fences for lines! Add a minecart to the track and six fences to your base. Now you and your friends can line up for the ride of your life!

EXPERT TIP!

TAKE A SPOOKY SPIN

Now that you've honed your roller coaster skills, how about taking your ride underground? Create a truly creepy ghost train complete with cobwebs, red-eyed spiders, zombies, and lava pits!

STEP 12

Every roller coaster needs an entrance to set the mood. This one has four chiseled sandstone blocks for the pillars and five purple and orange wool blocks for the lintel. The finishing touch – two torches and a couple of gruesome creeper heads!

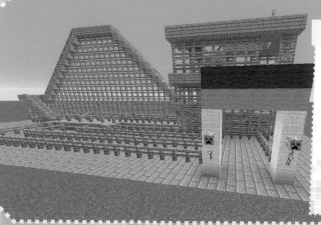

Now that you are master of all the Minecraft builds you survey, it's time to build an awesome castle. Show off your new skills with a stunning tower and an interior fit for a Minecraft monarch and a host of royal subjects. There's plenty of room to develop this build further, too, by turning the turrets into eight small rooms once you've finished your castle.

ON TOP OF THE WORLD

CASTLE

DIFFICULTY
MASTER

BUILD TIME
3 HOURS +

MATERIALS

STEP 1

First, lay your castle floor with a 20x20 oak-wood-plank square. Add a 16-plank L-shape at each corner, as shown. These are the basis for four royal turrets that will make your castle really stand out.

STEP 2

Next, build cobblestone walls along the edges of your floor. These should be nine blocks high. Leave a four-block gap for the entrance. Build the walls of the four corner turrets 11 cobblestones high.

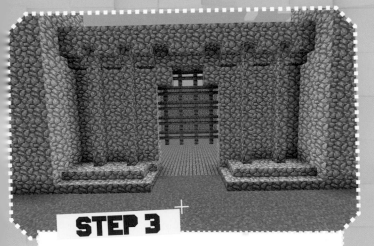

STEP 3

On either side of your entrance, build steps of cobblestone and cobblestone stair. Create four mossy cobblestone-wall columns with a 14-cobblestone row above and eight stairs underneath the row as shown. Add a portcullis made from dark oak fence and a cobblestone in each top corner.

STEP 4

On the other three sides of the castle, build more steps from cobblestone and cobblestone stair. Add six mossy columns with a 14-cobblestone row above and eight cobblestone stairs underneath for decoration, just like you did for your castle entrance.

STEP 5

Build a cobblestone roof one block down from the top of your castle walls, as shown. Add corners to the inside of your turrets with L shapes made from three cobblestones. These should be two blocks high.

EXPERT TIP!

ROYAL COLORS

Brighten up your castle by building with hardened clay blocks, which come in a range of colors. You can also give some colorful glamour to your castle by adding stained glass windows.

STEP 6

Add cobblestone wall to the edges of your castle walls, as shown. Add more wall to the inside edge of each of your turrets and use cobblestone to create a roof for each. Now it doesn't matter if it rains!

STEP 7

Make a 6x6-block hole in the center of your roof. Then build walls seven cobblestones high around this hole. You now have the base for your castle's central tower.

STEP 8

Build four cobblestone squares on top of your base, each one two blocks smaller than the last. Your castle is really starting to take shape! Features like this are an indication of the wealth and power of the royalty inside.

STEP 9

Extend your 6x6 square to create a 10x10 overhang. Build six ever-decreasing stone brick slab squares on top of this, followed by a square of cobblestone. Add cobblestone wall to each corner and a pyramid of stone brick slab with a 4x4-slab base.

STEP 10

Build steps from cobblestone and cobblestone stair around the base of the tower. Add cobblestone stair to the underside of the overhang at intervals, as shown, and build columns in between the gaps left by the cobblestone stair on each side.

STEP 11

Time to decorate! Place banners on cobblestone blocks in each turret. Add two banners and torches on either side of your central tower. Finally place four banners and six torches at your entrance, as shown.

STEP 12

Inside, build a wooden platform six planks wide and eight planks long against the back wall. Cover this with slabs. Add six planks and four slabs at the front. At the sides, add three steps up to flooring two slabs wide. Decorate with torches, canvases, and banners.

STEP 13

Now lay a walkway along each wall. Continue laying slab into each turret to create a second floor. Build a safety rail using planks and fence. Decorate with torches, banners, and canvases. Finally lay some royal red carpet.

STEP 14

Craft a throne to show all those endermen who's boss! Build a 4x2-slab base, add a slab at either side with a four-plank row at the back and two slabs on top. Finish it off with two red carpet tiles.

STEP 15

Craft a banquet table from oak wood plank and benches from oak wood stair so your subjects can join you for a royal feast. Add torches so they can see what they are eating and drinking.

STEP 16

All the best castles need a moat! Dig four blocks down and seven blocks out from your castle. Lay cobblestone at the bottom of your ditch, extend your castle down by three cobblestones, and then add water.

STEP 17

Craft your bridge from birch wood slab. It should be four slabs wide and eight long. For the finishing touch, add pillars of cobblestone and two blocks of cobblestone wall on the grass at either side.

EXPERT TIP!

GREEN WITH ENVY

Once your castle is complete, add a grandiose garden around it. Check out some of the world's most famous royal gardens for inspiration – Versailles is a perfect example.

GLOSSARY

The world of Minecraft is one that comes with its own set of special words. Here are just some of them.

« BIOME »

A region in a Minecraft world with special geographical features, plants and weather conditions. There are forest, jungle, desert and snow biomes, and each one contains different resources and numbers of mobs.

« COLUMN »

A series of blocks placed on top of each other.

« DIAGONAL »

A line of blocks joined corner to corner that looks like a staircase.

« HOTBAR »

The selection bar at the bottom of the screen, where you put your most useful items for easy access during Survival mode.

« INVENTORY »

This is a pop-up menu containing tools, blocks and other Minecraft items.

« LAY »

To put down a floor covering, like a carpet.

« LINTEL »

A horizontal structure that spans the top of a doorway or window.

« MOB »

Short for "mobile," a mob is a moving Minecraft creature with special behaviors. Villagers, animals and monsters are all mobs, and they can be friendly, like sheep and pigs, or hostile, like creepers. All spawn or breed and some – like wolves and horses – are tamable.

« OVERHANG »

Part of a rock or a structure that sticks out over something else below.

« ROW »

A horizontal line of blocks.

« TURRET »

A small circular tower that is part of a castle or another large building.

FURTHER INFORMATION

BOOKS

Minecraft: Guide to Creative by Mojang AB and The Official Minecraft Team. Del Rey, 2017.

Minecraft: Guide to Exploration by Mojang AB and The Official Minecraft Team. Del Ray, 2017.

Minecraft: The Complete Handbook Collection by Stephanie Mitton and Paul Soares Jr. Scholastic, 2015.

WEBSITES

Visit the official Minecraft website to get started!
https://minecraft.net/en-us/

Explore over 600 kid-friendly Minecraft videos at this awesome site!
https://www.cleanminecraftvideos.com

INDEX